The Flute Player

Shawn Mihalik

Asymmetrical Press
Missoula, Montana

Published by Asymmetrical Press, Missoula, Montana.

Dance lessons sold separately.

Library of Congress Cataloging-In-Publication Data
The flute player / Shawn Mihalik — 2nd ed.
ISBN: 978-1-938793-12-7 eISBN: 978-1-938793-13-4 WC: 20,211
1. Dragons. 2. War. 3. Young Adult. 4. Death. 5. Music.

Cover design by Colin Wright
Printed in the U.S.A.
Formatted in beautiful Montana

Author info:
Website: asymmetrical.co/shawn
Email: shawn@asymmetrical.co
Twitter: @shawnmihalik

ASYM
METR
ICAL

For E.B.

We are the music makers,
And we are the dreamers of dreams.
—Arthur O'Shaughnessy

"And then she woke up."
I suppose there are worse endings.
—Neil Gaiman, *The Sandman #16*

The Flute Player

NOT SO VERY FAR AWAY *from here, and yet not so near that one could easily find them, there lie mountains. And these mountains, being cold and covered as deep as one can tell with snow and ice, were the perfect place among which to hide a civilization. Many thousands of years ago, someone decided that it would be in the best interests of all the world were he to do just that.*

If we were to go searching for this civilization—that is assuming that we had a map of sorts and pre-acquired near-precise knowledge of where this civilization was and how exactly to get there—we would likely not survive the journey anyhow. If we first found the mountains among which this whole different world hides—and I must point out once again that these mountains themselves are really not so far away. So close are they in fact that if you were to look out your bedroom window right now you could probably see them in the distance. Go ahead and do it now. Look out your window. Do you see them? Trust me, they are there, but only if you look in a special way.

Anyway, if we found these mountains and traveled to them, we would then of course have to climb them. We would probably fall while climbing, and if the fall did not take our life, then the fear of falling again would certainly keep us from a second attempt. But if we did not fall, or if we were very brave or foolish, if we instead made it to the top of the sheer cliffs that make up our side of the mountains, then the next step would be to face the giant ice beasts that guard the entrance to the lava caves. Having once fought a single ice beast, I can honestly say that there is no way we would be able to fight an entire pack of ice beasts and live.

You see, ice beasts are huge, ferocious creatures with rows and rows of sharp crystalline teeth and many hands and fingers that sport razor-like shiny claws. The fur of an ice beast is so pure and white that it is impossible to see it among the snow. One might think that he is alone until the first ice beast pounces, but by then it is usually too late to think anything at all, for ice beasts are quite hungry.

But if we did manage somehow to shatter the glass horns upon the backs of the ice beasts, which would not kill them, only stun them for a little while, then we could proceed into the lava caves, where the scalding heat and fire would burn us instantly into nothing more than unfeeling cinders.

On the other side of the caves that we could never make it through, we would finally be getting close to our destination. The Grand Ocean would of course still be quite a hindrance to the progress of our journey, but knowing what we know of the journey, we would have had the forward thinking to bring a boat. This boat would also have been reduced to ash within the fire caves or eaten by the ice beasts or dropped from the snowy cliffs, but this is beside the point. With our boat we could traverse the Grand Ocean, dodging the sea monsters and the sharks and the deceitfully cuddlesome poisonous eel. Perhaps a kind orca might even give us a boost with his mighty tail so that we could make our destination faster.

And then we would be there. We would be in a different world, not so very far away from our own.

However, since it would be entirely impossible for us to make the journey, I shall simply have to take you there now myself. I know a shortcut. For you see, I have survived the journey myself, and once one makes it to the secret civilization, one needs only to think about it to go there again. Think now, close your eyes halfway, and we shall go.

We can see the world now, past the snowy cliffs and the summits of the ice beasts, through the smoldering lava caves and across the infinite Grand Ocean. It is a village, small but warm and pleasant. Three children are playing in the hills while the adults are waiting eagerly for the flute player to play his nightly melody . . . .

"THIS WAY," SAID OLIVER, CALLING to his friend Will across the bright green pasture. "I think he's hiding by the oak tree." The two boys laughed as they ran, their voices a youthful jubilee, their sandy blonde hair blowing in the wind like dry blades of grass. They were playing a game of hide-and-seek, and Oliver, whose hiding place behind the stones Will had just discovered, had offered to help find the third boy in exchange for a pardon.

"He's not here," said Will, walking slowly around the tree's massive trunk.

"He must be," said Oliver. "I know I saw him run over here while you were counting." They both walked around the trunk in opposite directions, only to meet up on the other side.

Oliver rubbed his forehead. "I don't understand. I know he came this way—"

"Hey, guys!" came a voice not too far away. "Over here."

Both boys looked to see their friend by the pond, standing on the dock that they had declared "base" at the start of their game, his hand held high and a mischievous smile on his face as he waved mockingly.

Immediately, Will turned to Oliver and tapped him on the shoulder. "You're it," he said with a grin.

"Hey, that's not fair," Oliver protested. "You promised not to tag me."

"Yeah," replied Will, "but only if you helped me find Thomas, and you didn't help me find Thomas."

"But I tried," said Oliver. "And it's not my fault that he changed hiding spots."

"That doesn't matter. A deal's a—" Will said, but his words were cut short by a thud and a splash. Both boys turned to see that Thomas was no longer standing on the dock. In fact, they couldn't see him anywhere at all.

"Thomas," breathed Oliver, breaking into a run. He saw his friend struggling in the pond, flailing his arms wildly, splashing cool water in every direction. His head failed to stay above the surface for more than a few seconds at a time. "Thomas!"

"What's happened?" asked Will as he arrived at the dock behind Oliver.

"Run to the village square and get help. Go now!"

Oliver knew that Thomas didn't know how to swim. None of the children in Drommar were taught to swim when they were young for fear that curiosity might draw them into the Great Ocean and they might be devoured by the monsters that lived there. Thomas continued to struggle in the water, and Oliver had no idea what he could do to help his friend. "Thomas!" he called, his voice desperate. "Don't worry. It'll be okay. Will's bringing help."

For at least a minute and a half Thomas somehow managed to continue bringing his head above the water, to gulp air into his lungs again and again, but his muscles were small, fatiguing quickly, and eventually Oliver's friend disappeared beneath the surface. The water grew still.

Tears were streaming down Oliver's face by the time help arrived minutes later. Will appeared, a swarm of adults running up behind him, Oliver's own father in the lead. Oliver's father ran across the dock and dove headfirst into the water, disappearing into the hydrous darkness. Oliver held his breath for an eternity before the man resurfaced, the child in his arms.

He swam to the dock, handing the boy to the village's best doctor, who was waiting for him at the edge of the dock with a medicine bag. The doctor lay the motionless body down and pressed his ear to the boy's chest. He wasn't breathing.

Oliver could see in the waning light that Thomas's face was blue and that his lips were cold. The doctor placed his mouth to Thomas's, breathing air into the boy's lungs, but there was no response. He tried again. And again and again and again. He pounded on the boy's chest with growing ferocity, knowing fully the importance of this child's place in the village. He breathed into his lungs again. Pounded again. Breathed again. Pounded. Breathed. Pounded. Breathed. The doctor continued, and the boy's chest and shoulders shook with every ministration, but it was only reflex, and Oliver knew his friend, the flute player, would never play again.

OLIVER AWOKE GASPING, STRUGGLING FOR several moments to take a complete breath. Sweat soaked his brow, although he didn't feel particularly warm inside his room. Noticing that there was not yet any sunlight peeking through his window, Oliver hoped for a moment that it was still early, that he may be able to rest for several more hours, but after wiping his eyes and looking over at the old clock on the room's single shelf, he realized that it was indeed time for him to awaken. He yawned, tired and knowing that he would be that way for the remainder of the day.

There was a knock on the door, and though it was not sudden—it came at the same time every day—Oliver's heart skipped a beat. He took several deep breaths. "Come in," he called.

His father, a tall man with longish dark hair, a clean-shaven square jaw, and cold hard eyes, entered the room. It was not always his father who opened the door. Sometimes one of the servants would be given the task of alerting him to the morning hour. Other times one of the chefs would do it. No one, save Oliver himself, seemed to mind starting the day so early—it was of course a great honor to wake him.

"Good morning," his father said, his voice deep and dry. "The sun will soon emerge from behind the mountains. Come. Breakfast is ready."

Oliver yawned again and followed his father out the door. When he reached his dining room—the entire cottage belonged to Oliver, at least technically, ceremonially—he found a pot of ginger-mint tea and two black ceramic mugs waiting on the table. Oliver sat across from his father, who took the pot and poured a spot into each mug, giving one to Oliver and sipping from the other one himself. "Have you written a new song for this morning, son?"

"No," replied Oliver, shaking his head, loudly swallowing the contents of his cup. The tea warmed his throat, nearly burned his tongue. "Nothing new. I'll just play the Rising March again."

His father's brow furrowed and he curled the corners of his lips downward. "The Rising March? No, no good. You've played that twice already this week. You must play something else."

Oliver nodded.

Two servants, both women about his father's age, brought breakfast—a selection of eggs, gathered that morning no doubt, warm rolls with honey, and bacon, also likely slaughtered and prepared that very morning. After the second servant finished placing the bacon before them on the table, the first reappeared, offering glasses of orange juice. Oliver's father accepted it gratefully, and Oliver, after a moment's hesitation, reached for a cup as well.

Father and son ate in silence. Only the awkward sounds of china and silverware clanking together, the subtle scrape of food being pushed around their plates, and their quiet mastication, filled the small house.

*****

It would have been day always in the village, were not one side of the mountains taller than the other, but because they were, the sun spent half of its counter-clockwise cycle around the village behind the larger portion, effectively blocking its light. At the moment, however, that very sun was slowly beginning to emerge from the right side of the taller mountains, shining its golden rays upon the village of Drommar. And this light brought with it the start of the day for all who lived there.

Some had awoken early just so they could gather in the square before daybreak, anxious to share the privilege of being present for the morning song. Most, especially those with large families and young children, usually found it too difficult to do so and instead opened their shutters so that the music would find its way to their ears in the comfort of their own homes.

On this particular morning, only about a hundred or so had gathered in the square, but there would certainly be many more when evening approached. All looked up in awe even though they had seen the sight many times before, and some cheered, although not too loudly, when Oliver was led by his two guides to the stage directly in the center of the village square. They quickly disappeared, however, when he opened the elegantly crafted wooden box that one of the guides handed to him. From inside it he pulled out a golden flute, which he placed delicately to his lips.

As Oliver began to blow into the lip plate, his fingers dancing deftly across the instrument, all the listening residents of Drommar found themselves swept away. They forgot their lives for a moment, abandoned all fear, every thought and troubling notion carried away on the back of the breathtaking melody.

And then, fluidly, the joyful tune changed to one of laconic sharps and flats. For the briefest of moments, melancholy, sadness, hopelessness entered the hearts of all who listened. And but one might only have imagined these fleeting feelings, for suddenly the notes were bright and high again, as if they had been all along.

The song lasted only minutes, and then Oliver, one guide in front of him and one behind, was led back to his home, leaving the villagers to begin their day.

"Can I talk to you, son?"

Oliver looked up from the sheets of paper spread out in front of him. His father was standing in the doorway just as he had been that morning, only this time the doorway led not to Oliver's bedroom but his writing room. Oliver nodded, laying the stylus that he was holding in his right hand on the floor.

"The village has been sad today," his father said.

Oliver blinked. "Why?"

"You know why. And therefore you know that that is not the real question, my son. The question is: why are *you* sad?"

Oliver looked away. He picked up the stylus again and began to make broad strokes across the paper. "I'm not sad."

His father sat on the floor, although far from him. "Everyone heard your song today, Oliver. There was sadness in it."

"It is my song," said Oliver. "I am the flute player. I am allowed to play as I like, be it sad or joyful."

"But that sadness greatly affects everyone else. I have spoken to many in the village today, and all say that their thoughts were tired and clouded this morning."

"They should sleep more."

His father ignored the remark. He brushed a long lock of

dark hair from his face, smoothing it back with the others. He rubbed his strong chin. "You know your responsibility, my son."

Oliver looked up from the papers. "Then I will play a happy song tonight. Will that please them?"

His father leaned forward. "A *new* song?"

Oliver was quiet for a moment. "Yes."

"Is that it? May I see it?" His father gestured to the sheets of paper on the floor.

Oliver shook his head. "No. It's . . . it's not quite finished yet."

But his father had already pulled the papers away. As he shuffled through them, his brown eyes narrowed and his ears pulled back against the sides of his head. "There is nothing written here," he said, his voice rising. "There is nothing written on any of these."

Oliver gazed at the floor. He shrugged, fiddling with the fabric of his trousers.

"Surely you have not been wasting your time?"

Oliver shrugged again.

His father took the stylus from the floor and forced it into Oliver's hand. "You must write music."

"I have nothing about which to write," Oliver replied, dropping the stylus, his hand limp.

"What are you talking about?" His father's voice was a low growl.

Oliver stood up, so that he now towered over his father, who was still sitting. "I have been doing this for nearly ten years now, playing my flute in the morning, playing again at night. I don't want to do it anymore. I cannot do it any longer."

Oliver's father stood up, his jaw tightening and the veins in his neck and forehead popping. "You know that you must."

"Then give me something about which to write, about which to play. Let me spend time among people. Among friends."

"That," he paused, "is impossible."

Oliver raised an eyebrow. "Why?"

"Don't be stupid, son. Remember Thomas."

"Of course I remember. I remember that he was allowed friends. *I* was his friend. And William. I've not seen William in years."

"Maybe," Oliver's father said, "if you hadn't been his friend, I wouldn't have had to drag his lifeless body from the pond."

The words stung, but Oliver knew his father—it wasn't as if they hadn't had this conversation before—and had anticipated the cruelty. "And yet," he replied, betraying none of the pain he felt, "Thomas's music was always joyful. I wonder, what would it have been like had he been shut away like I am?"

"Thomas's music was cheerful because he knew his place in this world. Without him, everyone would have drowned in the troubles that life dumps upon us. The music of the flute player allows us to escape those troubles, even if only for a little while, and it is your responsibility to make that happen."

"I know my responsibility, father, and yet it is not mine, is it?" Oliver said. "I was given no choice."

"Don't be ungrateful. It's not just a responsibility. It's a privilege. You bring honor to our family when you play."

"What family?" Oliver said. "I bring honor to *you*. Mother's been gone forever, and nobody knows who I am. But as long as your son is the flute player, you get your place on the council. You get your house and your servants and your women. And what about me?"

Oliver's father chuckled, an act entirely devoid of humor. "What about *you*? Son, do you realize how selfish you sound?

You get this house, your *own* servants. And when have you ever wanted for any material possession? Trust me, son, and trust the wisdom of your elders."

Oliver's voice grew louder. His hands clenched into fists. "Your *wisdom*? *Your* wisdom?"

But his father dismissed Oliver's anger with a wave of his hand. "The discussion is over," he said, spinning on his heel. "Now, write a song for tonight. Something happy." He left, closing the door firmly behind him.

Oliver listened as his father moved away from the door and heard him issue orders to the servants that Oliver was not to be bothered, not even for his supper. He sat on the floor again. He picked up the stylus and touched it to the paper, only to find that the ink had run dry.

THAT NIGHT, AFTER THE SUN had disappeared behind the tall mountains, Oliver rose from his bed. He had, per his father's wishes, played a cheerful tune that evening, never wavering from the notes on the paper, but he didn't honestly believe anybody had been fooled by it. Oliver hadn't even written the song in question. In truth, Oliver hadn't written a melody at all during his almost-decade as the flute player. Instead, when he really needed a happy song to play for the villagers, he would choose one that Thomas had written when he was young. And Thomas had written so many before his death that there existed scores of songs no one had heard. And even though Thomas had been so young, the songs were beautiful.

The song that Oliver had chosen that evening was called "The Magic Flute," and according to the notes that Thomas had scrawled across the sheet music, it had something to do with a man named Wolfgang. While playing the song for the crowd, Oliver had tried to picture this Wolfgang, hoping to feel the same joy Thomas might have felt when he first wrote it, but was unsuccessful.

Truthfully, Oliver did not consider himself to be an

exceptional flute player in any way, and he often wondered why the elders had chosen him to be Thomas's successor. They probably asked themselves the same question every day, and likely his father's sly words and earnest petitions were the only reason. Oliver could *play* the flute—Thomas himself had taught him. Give him a piece of sheet music, and he could easily move his fingers to form the corresponding notes. Where he paled in comparison to the flute players of the past was in his ability to *compose*. He had spent many hours—probably the equivalent of many days—reading the music of The Great Flutists of Drommar. Each and every composition seemed inspired, a feeling that Oliver never knew when he tried to write. Some of the music of the past felt as if it had been about specific individuals, while others seemed to represent events that had never happened, and still more appeared to be the product of all sorts of silliness and fun. But all of it was beautiful and human.

Certainly all the flute players before him had possessed an ability that Oliver himself did not. They knew musical theory; he knew musical theory. They knew inspiration; he knew only emptiness.

Oliver closed his eyes as he lay in bed, pondering the past, seeking the Muse. He pushed aside the thoughts that troubled him and opened his ears, hoping to catch an audible glimpse of the music that the world itself produced. Listening, he could hear the peaceful chirping of crickets rubbing their legs together as they called their friends. He heard the hogs squealing, oblivious as they were to the disturbance their obnoxious screeching caused, oblivious still that they might be but bacon in the morning. Oliver listened even harder, opening up not only his ears, but his soul, and he could hear the surf far off in the distance, beyond even the hills and the forest that surrounded the village. Certain that he was growing tired and his ears were playing tricks on him, Oliver thought he heard the snarling of the sea monsters and the ice beasts across the ocean.

And he could hear a woman—a girl?—screaming.

Oliver sat up. He strained his ears, alert now. Surely he was exhausted. Maybe he'd even begun to cross that line between wakefulness and sleep, where the mind... But there it was again, the desperate cries of a frightened young lady. He could hear it clear as day or night. He bolted from his bed, throwing the bedcovers to the floor and yanking on the door handle. Oliver had never tried to open his bedroom door at night before, but he should have realized that it would be locked. It *was* something his father would do.

Fortunately, his father's apparent need to protect his son did not benefit from too much forethought. Oliver's window had no lock, only two easily opened shutters.

Ignoring any concerns of safety, Oliver climbed out the window and fell onto the grass below, landing hard. He stood, brushing himself off, ready to ask what was happening. He was puzzled, however, when he saw that the streets of the village were empty. Not a soul was in sight. How could no one be reacting to the poor woman's cries? Couldn't they hear it? Couldn't they *feel* it?

It was clear to Oliver that the sound was coming from the direction of the hills, so without a thought he ran that way, oblivious to the fact that his feet were bare and he wore nothing but an unbuttoned shirt and thin cotton shorts. The air was cool, brisk, but he hardly noticed.

As Oliver made his way over the hills, the cries grew quieter, although they were still clear. Oliver had not traveled farther than his cottage or the village square in many years, and he had all but forgotten about the hillside. Now, though, he saw the stones where he would often hide during games when he was younger. And the large tree, in the final years of its life after standing tall for centuries, reminded him of one game in particular. The cries for help grew louder once again.

Oliver continued to follow them, running—sometimes slowing to catch his breath—for what seemed like forever. Then he paused. He'd reached the edge of the forest, and he couldn't help but notice the darkness within. He hesitated, but only for a moment.

Breathing deeply, Oliver stepped into the trees. Suddenly, he was engulfed in silence and clamor at the same time. His heart began to beat faster. His brow grew slick. And then he jumped, startled, as, without any warning, a sort of wooden podium appeared, and behind the podium stood a short, frumpy man. The man wore no clothes, save for glasses, but a flower was pinned to his chest. The man looked down, catching sight of his nakedness. His face, stricken with horror, dissolved just as suddenly as it had appeared, followed by his body and then the podium.

Oliver squinted, frightened, confused. There came a snarl from his right, and he turned just in time to see a tree burst into flames.

"I warn thee: Stand back!"

Oliver staggered backward as a man in glistering silver armor emerged from behind the flaming tree. The man waved a sword in front of him. "Do not worry. I will protect thee."

This man must have come from the village, Oliver thought, where there were a few law-enforcement officers, and although their services were rarely needed, they wore armor similar to this.

The officer must have heard the girl's cries and come to investigate.

"Protect me from what?" Oliver asked the man, ready for answers. Sensible, reasonable answers.

What he got instead was a laugh, and then, and the man's voice was deep, "Why, from the dragon, of course."

Indeed, a massive creature loomed before them.

Oliver marveled at the sight. He knew of sea monsters, and ice beasts, but this creature fit no description he had ever heard. Its face was long and serpentine, its mouth filled with rows of razor-like teeth. It had at least four legs that Oliver could see, although the majority of the beast's body was obscured by the trees, so it may have had far more; in fact, there was no telling how long the creature was. The parts of its body that Oliver could see, however, were covered with rocky scales that glistened in the light of the fire. The beast was as tall as the forest itself.

The monstrous creature let out a terrifying roar, and fire flew forth from its mouth, alighting the canopies of several nearby trees. Oliver felt the heat and thought his skin might blister.

"I don't understand," Oliver said stepping backward.

"The dragon," answered the soldier, "has been terrorizing the nearby village for many years, but I, Sir Lawrence the Honorable, shall strike him down."

"But the village is fine," Oliver said. "And I've never seen this creature there."

"Hush," said the man. "Neither speak nor worry anymore." A white horse materialized—or had it been there the entire time? —and the man climbed effortlessly onto its back. The man raised his sword, thrusting it forward, and lifting his head high. He reached for the helmet on his head and pulled a protective mesh mask down across his face. "I ride!"

Oliver watched the horse bolt valiantly toward the dragon, but in an instant the entire ludicrous scene disappeared, and Oliver was alone in the darkness once again, accompanied only by the trees, which appeared untouched by the fire, and the young woman's cries for rescue, sounding closer than ever.

Oliver was unsure of what he should do. For an instant, he doubted his sanity. But then he ran again, ignoring the pain shooting through his bare feet as they were cut and scraped by rough forest floor, toward the cries. When he reached a small clearing, he saw something arguably stranger than anything he had seen before.

There, on the other side of the clearing, was a burning structure. It was obviously a vehicle of some sort—it had wheels and what looked like a large area for cargo in the middle—but it was unlike a rickshaw or a wheelbarrow in that the entire thing was made of metal and painted a light blue. The front end was clearly damaged, smashed, and the rear was on fire. And sitting in the cargo compartment, shouting, was a girl.

Frozen for only a moment, Oliver ran to vehicle. "Don't worry," he called through the cracked glass. "I'm going to help you!"

He saw what looked like a latch attached to the side of the vehicle. He pulled on it, but it wouldn't budge. He yanked as hard as he possibly could. The latch came off in his hand. Dropping the latch, Oliver ran his hand along the smooth blue surface. It was warm—but not hot, not yet—and his fingers found what he was looking for. The door-seam was too thin for Oliver's fingers, but there had to be something nearby he could use to pry it open.

He turned, ready to run into the forest again, when the

young woman spoke. "No!" she cried, putting her hand on the window.

Oliver pivoted back to the young woman. He placed his hands on the glass, and they lined up perfectly with hers. He looked into her eyes, knowing the fear that she felt and seeing strength inside her at the same time. "I'll be back for you," he said, almost in a whisper. She heard him, however softly he may have spoken, and ceased her cries. She nodded.

Oliver didn't know how much time the girl had, but something told him he would have to be quick if he were going to save her. Nearly overwhelmed by urgency, he searched the woods for something—a branch, a stick—thin enough and strong enough to pry the door open. His mind raced.

He didn't understand what had happened tonight, and he wasn't sure that he ever would. The girl was on fire. Why? Where had she come from? Did the fire have something to do with that beast, the *dragon*, and if so, why hadn't the flames disappeared with the rest of them? But yet he'd heard the young woman's cries what must have been hours ago. How long had she been out here?

The forest floor was littered with sticks and twigs, but nothing sturdy enough for Oliver's needs. Surely, they'd all snap in two before he could get the door open. The branches on the trees were stronger, but he doubted any of them would fit. The crackling of the flames in the distance grew louder. He was running out of time. *She* was running out of time.

"Excuse me, good sir."

Startled, Oliver turned. Behind him once again stood the man in silver armor. He definitely wasn't from the village, Oliver decided.

"Excuse me," the man said again. "I'm sorry to trouble you,

but I seem to have misplaced my horse. Have you seen—? Wait a second. I *know* you. . . ."

"Yes," Oliver said. "We met a few minutes ago, but you disappeared. There was a dragon and—"

The soldier grabbed Oliver by the shoulders, shaking him. "Yes, yes, the dragon. I need to stop the dragon."

Oliver jerked his body away from the man's grasp. "You already stopped the dragon," he said. "Listen, I need your help. There's a girl back that way and she's in trouble. She's trapped. We need to help her—"

"No!" the man said. "I must find my horse. I have to stop the *dragon*!" The man pushed Oliver to the ground, running past him in the direction opposite where the young woman waited. The trees rustled behind him as he vanished into the woods.

Rubbing his lower back, Oliver stood up. He winced, but his lips curled into a self-satisfied smirk at the same time. He had what he needed.

Running back to the burning vehicle, Oliver saw that the flames had grown larger, spreading around the vehicle and into its interior. "Help," the girl called as he approached.

"I'm here. I'm here," Oliver said, trying to reassure her. "Move back." He took the sword he'd plucked from the armored man's belt when he'd pushed Oliver to the ground and plunged the blade into the crevice between the door and the rest of the vehicle. Fire licked at the side of the sword as he pushed the hilt inward toward the metal like a lever. The blue paint was beginning to blister and peel.

Oliver was not a strong young man, and his muscles ached as he pried at the door. He began to sweat, a symptom of both the heat and the exertion. The bottom of his trousers caught fire, and he swung his leg wildly as he pushed on the sword. He could see the young woman staring back at him. "Kick the door," he told her.

She did as he said. She kicked and he pried. He kicked at his flaming ankle with the opposite foot. Thousands of moments later, the door opened.

Later, the girl would tell Oliver the vehicle was called "Beetle." It was larger than any insect he'd ever seen.

Oliver pulled the girl from the vehicle, and they both stumbled to the ground. "We have to get away," she said, half standing and half crawling, pulling at his arm. Her voice cracked when she spoke. She yanked him forward, nearly ripping his arm from its socket. They reached the edge of the clearing and she shoved them both to the ground, shielding Oliver. "Cover your ears," she said.

He did, and she did the same, and they sat there like that on the forest floor, waiting.

When after several minutes nothing happened, they both looked up, only to see that the flaming vehicle was gone. "It disappeared," she gasped.

Oliver looked at her, grasped her arms to see if she was real. "You didn't," he said.

The young lady, breathing heavily, glanced around the woods. She looked at the sky, and her gaze settled on one point in the distance, where the sun was beginning to emerge from behind the tall mountains. "Hi," she said.

"Hi," Oliver replied breathlessly. He smiled weakly at the girl, mesmerized and deeply puzzled all at once. He hadn't had the chance to get a good look at her before—what with the life-threatening danger and all—but he did now. She was about his age, and he could tell because she held her lips, which sat almost as an elegant afterthought upon her face beneath her small, gently pointed nose and subtly striking blue eyes, in a way that conjured in one's mind the image of a small child, free and happy, warring with a heavy sadness and responsibility. It's how all young people at the cusp of adulthood hold their lips. In her face, which was framed by long, lightly curled locks of golden hair, Oliver saw the same heavy-heartedness that he often felt.

Realizing they still sat in the dirt, Oliver remembered himself and rose to his feet, extending a hand to her. "My name is Oliver," he said.

"I . . . I'm Alexandria." She took the offered hand, and Oliver noted that hers was slightly cold. Not exactly an icy cold or a frozen cold. More like a quiet cold. A lonely cold.

Oliver asked the obvious question as he pulled her to her feet, "Where did you come from?"

"I'm from Nantes," she said.

Oliver didn't know what Nantes was, which did not surprise him because as far as he knew, Drommar was all that existed, at least on this side of the mountains. "I've never heard of that," he told her.

"It's in western France," Alexandria said.

He stared at her for a moment. "France?"

"Where is *this* place?" Alexandria asked, looking at her surroundings once again.

"This is the forest," Oliver told her. "Drommar is just beyond the edge."

It was Alexandria's turn to not understand. "Drommar?"

"The village," Oliver clarified. "It's where I live."

"How did I get here?" Alexandria asked.

"I don't know." Oliver shrugged. "Don't you?"

Alexandria shook her head. "I don't remember. Everything is foggy."

"Maybe we should get you to the village," Oliver said. "My father—well, he's smarter than I. He may be able to help."

Alexandria nodded.

The girl moved unsteadily, still shaken and frightened by her arrival. Oliver himself was both frightened and excited; as far as he knew, nothing like this had ever happened before. He had heard stories of worlds beyond the sea, beyond the mountains, but they were fairy tales, always vague and unfounded. Thomas, however, had been particularly fond of them, constantly telling Oliver and his friends about the people who lived there, although he never claimed to have visited the other worlds himself.

Oliver felt a pang in his gut at the thought of his friend. Why did his father have to so cruelly bring him up the day before? Obviously, Oliver felt guilt over his friend's death. He felt it every day, but was there really anything Oliver could have done to stop it?

Alexandria started to trip as they walked, and Oliver slipped his hand around her shoulders to offer support. She didn't protest. In fact, she looked at Oliver and smiled faintly.

"Thanks," she said.

Her entire body shared the same cold that her hand did, Oliver realized. Thomas had been cold when he'd died. His face and lips had been blue, and his eyes had had a chilling emptiness about them.

Oliver shuddered and urged himself not to think about such negative things. The past was the past and could not be altered, so Oliver's focus belonged in the present. It was something his father often reminded him of, and Oliver couldn't help but acknowledge that there was, in fact, wisdom in it.

Where exactly had this girl come from? Had she really come from beyond the mountains? It certainly seemed likely, but if so, then how had she crossed the ocean with its beasts and monsters? And what of her burning vehicle—had she used that to cross the ocean somehow, maybe?—that had disappeared so suddenly just like everything else he had seen that night? Everything, that is, save for Alexandria herself.

Could his father really help? Oliver didn't know. The more he asked himself that question, the more Oliver began to wonder if his father would even be willing to help. It was daylight now, meaning Oliver had already been gone through the morning. He couldn't imagine the uproarious effect his absence might be having on the village. Were they worried about him? No one knew that he had gone. When he returned with Alexandria, would his father just consider this strange girl another danger, like friends and loved ones and the world itself? And if so, what would his father do about it?

"Why does the sun move like that?" Alexandria asked.

Oliver shook himself from his ruminations. They had been walking silently for sometime already, and Oliver had lost himself deep in thought. "Like what?"

"Like that." Alexandria pointed. "It's moving sideways. Like a halo."

"That's just how it moves," Oliver said. "I don't think anyone has ever really bothered to figure out why."

"Why not?" Alexandria asked.

"Because that's just the way it is," Oliver said. "It would be a waste of time to try and explain it, I suppose, time that could better be spent caring for the needs of the village, growing food, building houses, making clothes."

"You don't have any desire to find an explanation for things? Aren't you curious?"

"I guess," Oliver said. "I don't know. I'm curious about you. Probably more curious than I've ever been about anything."

"Where I'm from—"

"Nantes?"

"Not just Nantes," Alexandria said, "but across the whole world, it looks as if the sun is moving, getting higher in the sky as the day goes on, until noon, and then it starts to sink again, and it eventually disappears beyond the horizon, and we have night.

"But really," she continued, "It is the earth that is moving around the sun, and it only looks to us as if the sun itself is moving. And I know that because we have scientists who have spent hundreds of years exploring and studying, trying to learn and discover new things."

"Well," Oliver said, "That's *not* how the sun works. Not here. The *sun* moves around *Drommar*, and it's nighttime when it disappears behind the tall half of the mountains, and morning when it reappears on the other side. And," he added, "no one does much exploring here."

He could tell that she was listening to him and trying to understand, but she seemed skeptical. He realized then that her steps were no longer unsteady, and she was calmer than before. He slid his arm down from around her shoulders, trying to give her space, but she reached out and grasped his hand in hers. So he left it there, noticing that hers was not as cold as before.

It took them nearly two more hours to complete the walk back to the village, and Oliver wondered if it had taken him that long to travel from his room to the clearing deep in the woods where he had found Alexandria, trapped in her burning vehicle. It certainly hadn't *felt* like that long, and yet it had felt longer, and but at night it's hard to judge such things.

During the rest of the walk they continued to talk, although Alexandria seemed disinclined to reveal much about herself. Oliver understood—she was doubtless still frightened, even though she didn't show it—and didn't try to press her for information about herself or her world, even though he was deeply curious. Instead, he told her everything he could think of about Drommar, although he left out some details, like his own feelings about his father, for example.

He told her about his position as the flute player, but he found it difficult to convey the weight his responsibility carried.

"Why do you play?" she asked.

"Because it is what is required of me," Oliver replied. "There has always been a flute player in Drommar, for as far back as anyone can remember."

"But why *you*?" she asked.

"I was chosen," he said. "It's my role."

Alexandria nodded. "You enjoy it, then?"

Oliver frowned. "I want to."

"But you don't."

"Sure . . . sure I do," Oliver said. "It's what's required of me." And of course he was lying, but it's what he would have told any stranger.

"By whom?"

"What?

"Who requires it of you? Who requires you to play?"

Oliver thought about that—he had never thought about it before. His father? Everyone? But even if those were true, they sounded like ridiculous answers, even to him, so instead he ignored the question. "Honestly," he said, "all I do is play. I'm supposed to compose, too. Every flute player before me has composed their own music."

"But you don't compose," Alexandria said.

"I try," Oliver said. "But I'm not very good at it. So instead, I just play the music of the past and hope that the villagers don't grow bored with it."

"I'd like to hear you play."

For some reason he could not explain, Oliver wanted nothing more than to do just that, to play for her, but he didn't reply.

"Look," Oliver said, pointing into the distance. "That's it. That's Drommar."

He heard Alexandria gasp as she saw the breathtaking view before her. And it really was breathtaking. Oliver had lived in the village his entire life—it was the only world he knew—and he hadn't seen it like this, from so far away, in a long time.

They had just breached the edge of the forest and now stood upon the hills, overlooking the entire valley in which the village sat. Light wisps of smoke rose from several chimneys. People moved busily about the village, all working to accomplish their daily tasks, hoping the flute player would play them a song that night. Women worked with their daughters, some in the square selling goods, others in front of their homes, busy making those same goods—products like clothes and blankets, soaps and fragrances, canned fruits and jams—to sell in the square the next day.

Just beyond the village, on the other side of the valley, Oliver and Alexandria could barely make out the tiny forms of men tilling the fields of their farms, harvesting vegetables, and herding sheep and other animals. In other parts of the village, men and older boys worked vigorously to build new homes, stores, and cottages.

A bell tolled, and a large group of children poured from the doors of a building on the village edge. A few adults followed them, trying to keep order. Oliver hadn't been to the school in a very long time, not since he'd become the flute player.

"It's so beautiful," Alexandria whispered.

"Isn't it amazing?" Oliver said. "You know, it's funny, I haven't seen Drommar like this in years. I'd forgotten how big it is."

"It is amazing," Alexandria said.

Oliver tugged lightly on her sleeve. "Come on. Let's go see my father."

OLIVER SUGGESTED THAT THEY TRAVEL around to the side of the village before entering it in order to reduce the chances of coming into contact with any of the villagers. Fortunately, everyone was busy working, and they were able to avoid the notice of the few people that they did run across on the way to Oliver's cottage.

Once outside the cottage, Oliver put his hand on Alexandria's shoulder. "It would probably be best if you waited out here," he said. "I'll talk to my father first. I'm sure he's quite angry with me right now."

Alexandria nodded. "Don't leave me too long," she said.

Oliver assured her he wouldn't and nervously walked to the front of the cottage. He reached out to open the door, but changed his mind at the last second. He crouched low and tiptoed to the side of the building where his bedroom window was located. This way, he might be able to find his father before drawing the attention of any of the house staff.

He pulled himself up to the window, which was curiously still open, and climbed quietly through. Upon entering his room, he noted that his bed was still unmade, odd because it was one of the first things the house staff did every morning. He tiptoed to the door and held his ear against it, listening for any sign of commotion and finding none. He opened the door, which was unlocked, proving that at least someone had entered his room at some point during the day.

He walked through the door and into the main hall, surprised to find it entirely empty. He checked every room of the house only to find the entire place similarly devoid of life. The chefs were not cooking in the kitchen. The housemaid was not dusting the wooden furniture or mopping the tiles. Even his music room was as untidy as he had left it the night before, whereas normally the servants had everything organized and neatly laid out for him so he could begin pretending to compose after the morning song. It was as if the work had been abandoned.

Oliver heard a thud from the main hall, and he spun out of the music room and ran toward the source. "What are you doing?" he asked when he saw Alexandria standing in front of the entryway.

"I was nervous," she replied. "You've been in here a while, and you promised not to leave me outside too long."

"I'm sorry," Oliver said. "It's okay. Come on in."

"You have a beautiful house," Alexandria remarked, walking deeper into the main hall and shutting the door behind her. "Kind of empty, though."

"Yeah. Usually it's bustling with activity. Too much activity. Everybody trying to make me happy, I guess. But now, I have no idea where everybody is."

"Looking for you, maybe?"

"It's possible, but we didn't see anybody on the way here."

"Maybe—"

Just then, the front door flew open, and Alexandria stopped talking. Oliver quickly pushed her through the nearest doorway, into the kitchen.

"There you are. Where have you been?" It was Oliver's father, his features not those of relief or worry but of choler. When Oliver did not immediately reply, his father walked into the room and grasped him roughly by the shoulders. "Answer me."

"I . . . I was in the forest," Oliver said, shaken. "Where's . . . where are the servants?"

"I sent them home," his father said. "Fortunate for you, I've managed to convince everyone that you're not feeling well today. What were you doing? Why were you in the forest?"

Oliver shook himself from his father's tight grasp. "I was trying to sleep, but a girl was screaming for help. Nobody else heard her, so I had to—"

His father cut him off with a wave of his hand. "Stop. Do you have any idea what you could have done? The village could have been thrown into frenzy without your song this morning. I've had to lie to everyone, even my fellow elders."

"She needed my help," Oliver protested. "No one else would help her."

"This is not the time for games." his father said. "When are you going to learn to grow up and take responsibility?"

"I'm . . . how did you not hear her?" Oliver said. "Her name is Alexandria. She's standing right behind you."

Alexandria had stepped out of the kitchen. Oliver's father turned, stared at Alexandria for a moment, and then turned back to Oliver. "Enough of this nonsense," he said. He grabbed Oliver by the shoulder once again and pulled him violently into the music room. "You're staying here. No servants today. Just you, your ink and paper, and your instrument. Your stunt this morning was unacceptable."

Oliver's father turned from the room and shut the door, and Oliver heard the click of the lock being turned. "I'll come and get you when it's time for the evening performance," his father said through the door. "I suggest you be prepared. And play something good."

The front door of the cottage slammed loudly, and Oliver sat for several moments in stunned silence, confused and frustrated and angry.

Slowly, the lock turned again and the door swung open. Alexandria stood in the doorway. "That—" she started.

"Yeah." Oliver said.

Alexandria walked into the room and sat down on the floor next to him.

"I don't understand. He didn't even acknowledge you," Oliver said.

"I don't think he knew I was there."

Oliver looked at her. "What do you mean? He looked right at you."

"He looked right through me," Alexandria said. "I could see it in his eyes. He couldn't see me."

"But that's impossible," Oliver said. "I can see you clear as day."

"Maybe . . ." Alexandria began, but left the thought unspoken.

"Maybe what?"

"Maybe I'm crazy. Maybe none of this is real and I'm hallucinating."

"That's ridiculous," Oliver said.

"Is it?" Alexandria asked. "I'm in a world I've never seen

before—never even heard of—a world where the most revered figure plays the flute and the sun travels in circles."

Oliver frowned. "What's wrong with playing the flute?" he asked.

Alexandria's face softened. "Oh, don't take it like that," she said. "I just mean…well, what if I made you up?"

"You didn't make me up," Oliver said. "I'm real."

"And I'm supposed to take your word for it?"

Oliver shook his head. "No," he said. "I must be the crazy one. You can't be real. None of the other things were real."

"What other things?'"

"Your . . ." he hesitated, struggling to remember the word, "beetle wasn't the only thing that disappeared in the forest last night," Oliver said. He told her about the naked man and about the knight with the dragon. He told her how they all appeared and disappeared out of thin air.

"You see," he said. "If anyone is crazy it must be me. I'm hallucinating."

"If I'm a hallucination," Alexandria asked, "then why didn't I disappear like those other things?"

"Because I'm obviously still imagining you."

Alexandria pursed her lips together, nodding. "That *would* be the obvious answer wouldn't it?" She shook her head. "No," she said, "I'm definitely the crazy one. Except, well, I don't feel crazy."

"I don't feel crazy either."

They sat on the floor for several moments in silence, their heads low. "Okay," Alexandria finally said, "now what?"

Oliver looked up. "Are you hungry?"

"I don't actually know," she said. "But I suppose I could eat something."

"My father's not coming back until this evening, but neither is the kitchen staff." Oliver looked at her. "I don't know how to cook."

Alexandria smiled, and Oliver realized that no one had smiled at him like that in a very long time—the servants smiled but never sincerely, the villagers smiled only to themselves, and his father never so much as simpered. "I can cook," Alexandria said.

"Can you cook well? Because the kitchen staff is terrible."

And so Alexandria cooked—the cottage's kitchen was well-stocked with pastas, breads, fresh meats, fruits and vegetables, and it was unlikely that later anyone would notice the missing food—and while she cooked, Oliver returned to the composition room and sat once again on the floor. He thought briefly as he always did of trying to compose something new, and as he always did he decided not to even bother, because he would come up with nothing anyway, and he picked up some of the old books and leafed through them. He stared at the notes for some long time, but he didn't see them, and he wondered just what was happening and was he crazy and was she real and what was he supposed to do now? Alexandria appeared in the doorway and told him the meal would be ready soon. Oliver stood from the wooden floor, which creaked beneath him, and insisted on picking a few flowers for the table because it was what the servants did and what his mother used to do.

The air, which had been uncharacteristically warm this morning, had grown brisk throughout the afternoon, and Oliver shivered as he walked outside, and yet he found the coolness comforting. He glanced around, watchful for anyone who might be near the cottage, fearful that his brief outing might get back to his father, who believed that Oliver was alone in his music room preparing for the evening.

Oliver stalked quietly back to the gardens, and even here there were no servants tending the expansive variety of flora. He carefully examined the lilies and the Narcissi, leaning close to each and inhaling their aromas and flavors. He didn't know which flowers were supposed to be better than others, which scents or colors were considered preferable, but he supposed they all must be if someone took the time to grow them. He decided on hyacinths and picked several purple ones. He found a tall ceramic vase sitting on a bench near the edge of the garden and from the nearby pump Oliver filled it with water, and then he filled it with flowers. He rearranged the flowers, moving this one here and that one there, and he stood back and looked at his creation and decided it was good enough. He'd never had reason to beautify anything.

When Oliver reentered the cottage, he was struck by the scent of Alexandria's cooking. He hadn't eaten since dinner yesterday, and though he hadn't checked a timepiece, he knew it was well into the afternoon now. His stomach growled.

OLIVER TWISTED THE DELICATE NOODLES around his fork. Savoring the moment, he brought the fork to his mouth and ate, enjoying this mouthful just as much as he had the last. The pasta was the same pasta he'd been eating his entire life, bland and spongy, but the sauce, creamy and buttery and sharp and cheesy, was unlike anything he'd had before. He swallowed, picked up his glass of wine.

The wine, although there were many bottles of it stored in the cellar, was meant only for special occasions, and so the servants hadn't served any in sometime, because when was there ever a special occasion anymore in Drommar? And despite the fact that the house was his, the wine cellar was inaccessible to Oliver, locked and bolted and he had no key, but he'd managed to sneak down there a few months ago when, after a severe storm had caused some flooding, a servant had left it open for cleaning, and he'd taken two bottles, one white and one red, and kept them hidden deep in his wardrobe, and today he'd opened the red so that he and Alexandria could enjoy it with their meal.

"And what is this called?" Oliver asked, taking another bite of the pasta.

"Fettucini Alfredo," she said. "My mother taught me to make it, even though it isn't French."

"It's very good."

"I can tell you like it."

"So, I was thinking," Oliver said around another mouthful. "The way I see it, there are two possibilities about where you came from. The first possibility is that one of us is crazy, and it would have to be me who's crazy because if you're the crazy one then that means I'm not real, and I certainly remember being real, right? And the second possibility, and I like this one a lot more, is that you came from somewhere on the other side of the mountains."

"What's on the other side of the mountains?"

"I was hoping you could tell me."

THE WORLD ON THE OTHER side of the mountains is not a happy one. Right now, it is the seventeenth day of August 1943, and we find ourselves in Nantes, a city sitting on the Loire River in the west of France. Had we been here a day ago, we would have witnessed a horrifying event. We would have seen the cataclysmic effects of dozens of bombs falling from the sky upon thousands of frightened and innocent individuals. We would have been present as buildings were destroyed, streets were ravaged and desolated by fearsome explosions, and people were maimed and killed as those same explosions rocked their homes and businesses. Had we been here just three days ago, we may have seen a seventeen-year-old woman named Alexandria driving a blue Volkswagen Beetle down a dusty road near the riverbank. We would have witnessed the shock on her face as the ground around her and the sky above her exploded, forcing her off the road and into a burning tree.

ALEXANDRIA TOLD HIM ABOUT THE war, about Germany and Poland and France and the United States and all of it and how her brother was in the army and how her father and mother worried about him every day, and Oliver said that it all sounded so insane to him, so many people killing each other, and the thing was that Alexandria couldn't even really tell him what everybody was fighting for, although she didn't know if she actually didn't know or if she just couldn't remember, the same way she couldn't remember exactly how she had arrived in Drommar.

"What's the last thing you remember?" Oliver asked.

"Specifically?" She pursed her lips and scrunched her nose, her eyes drifting up and to the left. "I don't know. I guess I was . . . I don't know."

"But you remember everything. Like your life and your family and everything."

"Yeah."

"But if you don't remember how you got here, how are we supposed to help you get back? Nobody's ever made the trip across the ocean, let alone the mountains. Nobody's ever been beyond the woods. And we can't exactly ask for help, since apparently nobody else can see you. And, of course, I'm probably just crazy anyway."

Alexandria was quiet for several moments, they both were, and then she said, "What if I don't want to go back? What if I want to stay here?"

Oliver and Alexandria had only just finished cleaning the table and returning the house to its previous state when they heard the large front door begin to creak open. Oliver rushed into the music room while Alexandria quickly locked the door behind him.

Oliver's father once again paid no attention to Alexandria as he strolled right past her and unbolted the door. Oliver was sitting cross-legged on the floor, the mouthpiece of his golden flute raised to his lips.

Oliver made to stand, but his father motioned him to continue sitting and sat himself down on the floor next to him.

"Listen," Oliver's father said. "I wanted to apologize for the way I treated you earlier."

Oliver was quiet for a moment. "Okay," he said.

"No, it wasn't." his father said, even though that wasn't what Oliver had meant. "In fact, I've been thinking a lot about what you said yesterday, and you're right. You do deserve more freedom in this village. You are a grown man, and any man deserves freedom."

"Thank you," Oliver replied, surprised. "I appreciate you saying that."

His father nodded. "And so then of course you must also understand why I cannot grant you those freedoms."

Oliver stiffened. "That," he said, "I do not understand."

"Your responsibilities in this village are far greater than mine," his father told him. He glanced around the room, saw the sheets of music on the floor, and picked up several of them. "This," he said, waving the paper, "is the most important thing in the world. Everybody in this village faces monumental challenges. It's a part of life."

Oliver thought about the things Alexandria had told him about her world, about the war and the death, and he thought about how she couldn't even remember things and about how unfair that felt and how he was probably crazy, and he found himself growing angry, incredulous. Monumental challenges indeed. At that moment, Oliver noticed Alexandria standing in the doorway. When he saw her, she turned to leave, but with a nearly imperceptible motion of his head Oliver beckoned her to stay. Nodding, she entered the room and sat on the floor next to him.

Oliver's father continued without acknowledging her in any way. "Imagine," he said, "if you had disappeared this morning and something had happened to you. What if you had died, attacked by a wild beast? What if, because of that, nobody played for the people? Then we would have nothing to inspire us at the start of the day and nothing to relax us at the end. Soon, all our troubles and worries would build upon each other, stacking higher and higher and higher until the stack threatened to topple. We would be crushed beneath the weight of our burdens."

Oliver wanted to speak, to ask just how bad those "burdens" could really be, but his father kept talking.

"But you are responsible for preventing that. Nothing can ever be allowed to happen to you. Thomas died, remember that, and it could have been disastrous if not for you."

Oliver nodded. "I understand," he said dryly.

His father smiled, patting him on the shoulder. "Good," he said. "Now, it's almost time to play, but first, I thought we could share supper."

"I'm actually not hungry," Oliver told him. "I think I would rather practice a little more before the evening song."

His father smiled. "So you *do* understand the need for dedication. Very well. I'll be waiting for you outside. You will play in half an hour."

"I'm looking forward to it."

His father left and Alexandria said, "He doesn't seem so bad."

Oliver felt lost, but not alone.

OLIVER PLAYED HIS FLUTE THAT night, and he played it again in the morning. In fact, his routine returned to relative normalcy over the next few weeks. Every morning and every night he would play for the villagers, and every morning and every night the villagers would listen to him play.

At first, he spent most of his spare time, which was most of his time, working with Alexandria to discover what he could about her situation. He asked veiled questions of his father and various servants. He read some of the older journals, searching for references to similar phenomena. He found nothing, though, and eventually, they stopped searching, and she seemed to settle into a routine of her own.

After several days of experimentation, they had seemed to confirm that only he could see, hear, and feel her. And yet her actions did not go unnoticed among others living in the village. One day, while Oliver was working on a special project in his music room, he heard a loud crash from the foyer. Rushing to see what had happened, he found Alexandria standing near a bowl of fruit that lay in pieces on the ground, and one of the house maids entered from the kitchen and began to clean the mess, cursing to herself, a puzzled look on her face.

Oliver had offered to let Alexandria have his room and he would sleep in the music room, but they quickly realized that such a change would not go unnoticed among the house staff, so Alexandria insisted that she would find somewhere to sleep, and that he should keep his room for himself.

But Alexandria didn't sleep. It wasn't that she had difficulty sleeping or was insomniac, but that she quite literally didn't need to sleep, and when she tried, she said the experience felt pointless and wasteful. She tried several nights in a row, having fashioned a quite comfortable bed for herself in the house's loft where no one was likely to find it, but no matter how much she did during the day, exhaustion never set upon her and sleep never stole her away. And so they accepted this curiosity for now, and she spent her nights as she did her days, exploring or talking with Oliver for hours. When Oliver's father or a member of the house staff came to wake him in the mornings, it was often the case that he had been awake with her for hours already, engaged in conversation.

Unfortunately, it was rare for the house to be empty, so Oliver and Alexandria were not able to again share a meal like they had on that first day of her arrival. But there were nights when she would remain outside his room, wait for the staff to either leave or fall asleep, and then she would unlatch the door and they would run into the hills where she had hidden, unseen earlier that day, a bottle of wine and some fruits or cheeses or pastries she may have "borrowed" from one of the stands in the village. She once tried to sneak into an unoccupied kitchen and bake some treats herself, but she only succeeded in making a mess that lead to a village-wide hunt for the vandal who would shamelessly break and enter and destroy another's property.

During these nighttime outings, Oliver would point at the sky, which was almost always entirely clear, and explain the stars of the Drommar sky to Alexandria. That one was called this. Those ones were called that. She would listen with fascination, and she explained to him that she was entirely unfamiliar with this sky, that she recognized none of the constellations. She tried to find the North Star, hoping to find some clue as to Drommar's location, but all the stars were so impossibly bright that she found it impossible to pick out the brightest.

"What season is this?" she asked one night, as they lay on the cool grass, hands intertwined, gazing at the lights in the sky.

Oliver told her that he didn't know what a season was, and when she explained the concept to him, he told her that things never changed like that in Drommar. The weather was always temperate, mild, except for the occasional rainstorm. She explained winter, describing the cold and snow that accompanied it, and he told her that the mountains were cold and snowy, or so he'd heard.

And these nights, with the stars and the grass and the talking, began to occur more and more frequently until, nearly every night, Oliver and Alexandria would sneak out of the cottage and lay in the hills under the stars. Eventually, Oliver began to fall asleep under the stars, and Alexandria would lay next him, unable to sleep herself, and occupy her mind with other things.

Sometimes she would think about her past, about her family, and about the life that she had so seemingly quickly abandoned upon her arrival in Drommar. Or rather, she tried to think of it. Its memory had all but left her. Her parents' faces were reduced to shadows at the edge of her memory. The war, the violence, the conflict—just blips, just words. And maybe her world really was gone; maybe it didn't exist at all. And maybe she preferred it that way.

Or maybe—just maybe—it lay just beyond the mountains.

Of course, if she knew more about how she'd come to be here—in this world, on this hill, on this grass and with these people who couldn't see her—she may have been able to discern more about these things. But she didn't think she wanted to discern anything at all, and so she didn't even try.

Sometimes on these nights, she would roll over onto her side and watch Oliver sleep. He always positioned himself the same —lying on his back, his hands behind his head, eyes softly closed, nostrils flaring lightly as he inhaled deeply the fresh night air. Why could he see her, and why could nobody else?

She watched him sleep for hours, and she felt alone, but not lost.

IN THE VILLAGE BEYOND THE mountains and the sea, weeks have passed, but here in the ruins of a once thriving city, Alexandria has been in a coma for only days.

The hospital room is colder than it should be, and the lights, which hang low from the high ceiling on ropes of interwoven rubber-coated copper cord and electrical wire, swing left and right, and they haven't stopped swinging since the bombs rocked the city days ago and set the bloody things off on their pendular course, and for some reason no one has reached out and stopped them, and they flicker every few minutes, plunging the room into darkness, and the same happens contemporaneously in several other rooms and corridors and foyers throughout the old and vitiated building.

The man and woman sit quietly in two wooden chairs next to the bed, and the chairs are hard and uncomfortable, their backs rigid and stiff and their seats splintered, and the woman's head lies on the man's shoulder. Her eyelids are heavy, but she can't imagine closing them. The woman and the man have been here for days with the girl in the hospital bed—even if they wanted to go home, there's hardly a home left for them. There's hardly a home left for anybody.

The doctor enters the room. He's older and his hair is grey and his face is cratered and wrinkled and looks like tanned leather. He smells of cheap cigarettes, nicotine and tobacco and tar. His coat is not as white as it once was, and it's stained here and there with blood and mucus, some of it his own, but the stains are dry and permanent, and all the coats are dirty anymore, so why bother changing. He's German, and he calls them Fräu and Fräulein, but the thing is that he's lived in this city for a very long time, long before the war, and he's kinder to the Ashley's than any of the nurses or the other doctors, and they appreciate it very, very much.

The doctor holds a wooden clipboard in his left hand. He pulls a wooden pencil, a stub, from behind his right ear. He's only just sharpened it with a surgical knife. Before that, the graphite tip was dull and round.

The doctor checks the girl's heartbeat—his stethoscope barely works, and he taps on it lightly a few times before placing it on the girl's chest and neck and the inside of her wrist. He makes some notes on the clipboard with the freshly sharpened stub of a pencil. He nods. He shakes his head. He checks the intravenous drip, which hangs from a movable pole by the bed. It's almost empty. He makes another note. He shakes his head. He lifts the girl's head a little, fluffs her pillow. He pulls up one eyelid and then the other, and the blue eyes stare back at him.

The man, the father, smiles at the doctor, and the doctor smiles back but faintly. He tells them that he'll continue to do all he can, but supplies are running low and the military has promised support and supplies but who knows when. The father nods, his beard making a scratching sound as it rubs against his wool turtle-neck sweater. He holds his wife, her head still on his shoulder. The doctor leaves the room and in the hallway he takes a deep breath. Damn, but if he weren't almost out of cigarettes.

The mother and the father watch their daughter. She's

breathing and sleeping. Their son, a soldier, is already gone, and they cannot bear to lose her too.

OLIVER SAT CROSS-LEGGED ON the floor in his music room as he often did after performing the morning song. The difference between always and now, however, was that now Oliver felt like he was accomplishing something by sitting there in the center of his music room cross-legged on the floor. Papers were strewn about the room, hundreds of sheets of music, songs on parchment and liquefied wood chips. Many of the songs were songs of the past, written by other composers and players—he was studying them intensely—but some of the pages on the floor, including the one right in front of him now, *he* had written, and while he absolutely hated most of what he'd produced, there were a few pages of which he was almost proud.

He'd yet to play any of it in public, of course, and he still didn't think he ever would, but that was okay, because right now all that mattered was the writing and the fact that he was writing. In his left hand he held a feathered stylus that Thomas had made a long time ago. He dipped the pen in one of the large wells of ink that sat next to him on the floor—there were several colors: black for putting the first notes on paper, a deep sea green to draw out the ledger lines, blues and reds for changes and edits.

The nib dripped, splashing cerulean liquid onto the hardwood floor, and so he blotted it gently on the cuff of his pants, which were rolled up and covered in inks of every color. He placed the pen to the parchment on the first line of the third movement, crossing out a sharp and drawing over it with a natural. He altered several more notes in the line before moving on to the next. He set the pen down, sat back and stared at the page for several moments before picking up his wooden pan flute. This was a different instrument than the one he usually played for the villagers each day, but he'd been experimenting, and he liked the pan flute's delicate, hollow sound. He raised the instrument to his mouth, hesitated, dropped his hands back down to his lap.

"Well," Alexandria said. She'd been sitting in the corner of the room, reading, watching.

Oliver sighed. Suddenly unsure, he raised the pipes back to his mouth and began to blow, starting with the first line of the movement. The tempo was slow and the melody smooth and gentle, and as he played, it was almost like he could hear the song's unwritten, absent lyrics in his head. Still, it wasn't right. It was closer, but there was something missing, somewhere in the fourth line, maybe, something with the tremolo or the vibrato. The pitch was off, maybe. He played it again, feeling the vibrations in his sternum as he played. There.

He set the pan flute down and picked up the pen again. Wetted the nib. Placed it on the sheet music.

"That was good," Alexandria said.

"Almost," Oliver said. "Almost."

As he drew the notes, there was a tap on the door. One of the servants, a young cook, poked her head into the room. "Excuse me," she said. "Will you be taking lunch in here today, or in the dining room?"

Oliver kept writing. "No lunch," he said without looking up. "I'm not hungry."

It was raining in the afternoon, a hard rain accompanied by the drums of roaring thunder and frequent, intense bolts of blue-white lighting. The savage storm continued on into the evening, the sky flashing for hours and the *pat-pat-pat* of water on thatched roofs and into rapidly filling pails and barrels driving all but the bravest inside, and in some areas, the streets began to flood, but not excessively, and only in that way streets and eyes and hearts sometimes flood for just a little while before the waters and tears and pain recede and all returns to normal.

Despite the inclement weather, Oliver insisted on playing that evening. A month ago, his father probably would have had to force him to play, and even still Oliver would have refused, although of course he'd end up playing anyway. Tonight, though, it was as if the rains were *trying* to stop him from playing, but they couldn't, and he and two servants wandered out into the square wearing canvas parkas that held out the rain but that were also hot and uncomfortable, and he played a song that Thomas had started but not finished long ago, and Oliver had considered finishing the song himself, but it seemed inappropriate somehow, so he played only what was written. The square was mostly empty, and the music was difficult to hear over the clamor that was rain and thunder, but those few who were outside that evening heard the best they had in a very long time.

The storm finally began to let up a couple hours before midnight, and by the time Alexandria came to unlock and open Oliver's door, the rain had stopped all together. Oliver, exhausted and wet and cold, had fallen asleep quickly and deeply that evening, and he awoke groggy and yawning. He blinked.

"The rain stopped," Alexandria said. She held up a small brown wicker basket. "And I have tartlets. I made them myself this time."

Oliver sat up. "Tartlets?"

They could have used the front door or any of the side doors or the back door of the cottage, but they never did and weren't going to start tonight, and so they climbed through Oliver's bedroom window and fell each in turn quietly onto the ground only a few feet below, landing deftly on their naked toes. The grass was wet and cold and Oliver thought that maybe he should grab a blanket or quilt or something—something for them to sit on under sky and the stars—but Alexandria was already off, moving through the night and toward the usual place, and so he forgot about the blanket and just followed her, and they sat in the damp grass in the usual place and didn't mind.

Alexandria opened up the basket, reached in and pulled out two of the small pastries. Oliver took one and smiled and bit into it. She'd made it with cherry and blackberry and lemon, and she'd made it perfectly. The crust was flaky and buttery and melted in Oliver's mouth, and the filling was sweet but not too sweet, tart but not too tart, and after his first bite Oliver scarfed the rest down wolfishly.

Alexandria handed him another one, and a little abashed of himself, Oliver ate this one slowly, and while he ate he stared forward. From this spot on the hill one could see the entire village: there, right over there to the left, was the cottage and the garden, and a ways past that the school. It was all so quiet, asleep. Where was everyone? Oliver wondered, and of course it was something of a silly question. They were all in their homes and with their families, and in some of the houses the lights were still on, but in most the windows were dark, the occupants restful. As Oliver watched the village, he felt Alexandria's eyes on him, and he knew what she was thinking, and that comforted him.

After some time, Oliver turned toward her and smiled and wiped a crumb from the edge of his mouth. "So," he said, "you made these? They're delicious."

Alexandria returned the smile, looking a little embarrassed now herself. "Yes," she said. "I snuck into the bakery during the storm. The baker had gone, but he'd left the oven warm."

"Do you think he'll miss them, the baker? The ingredients, I mean?"

"Oh, probably. He always does, but it's kind of funny. He gets all frustrated and the flab on his cheeks and neck start to shake, and then he stomps outside into the street in front of the bakery and goes on and on about thieves and hooligans. He actually seems like a thoroughly unpleasant man."

Oliver had never met the man. When he was a child, though, the bakery had been run by a rail-thin elderly gentleman with big eyes and one of the kindest smiles he ever knew, and he'd always give Oliver and his friends a cookie or a turnover or cherry tart as they passed by on their way to school. But he'd passed away several years ago. Oliver had played the lament at the funeral, a solemn piece called simply "Threnody."

"And also," Alexandria said, "I left him a few of the tartlets on the counter."

Oliver laughed. "Good," he said. "I'll bet he can learn a thing or two from you. You're wonderful."

Alexandria blushed. "I'm not," she said.

"Oh, but you are. You're absolutely amazing."

"Thank you," she said.

Oliver leaned over and kissed her on the cheek. He started to move away, but her hand stopped him as she placed it gently on his face. "Your beard," she said.

Oliver hadn't shaved in over a week, and the stubble on his face was beginning to grow in thick and long, and there were flecks of red mixed in with brown. He put his hand on top of hers. "Yes?" he said.

"I don't know." She closed her eyes for a moment, opened them again. "I really don't know. I thought . . . I thought I remembered something, but it's gone."

"Something you knew before, you mean? About how you're here?"

"Yes, but . . . " She shook her head. "But it's gone again." She dropped her hand and lay back on the grass.

Oliver let go of a breath he hadn't realized he'd been holding and reclined back on the grass also. He nearly gasped as the wetness of the blades touched the back of his neck, cold on his bare skin, and but the sensation subsided, slowly, and he let his muscles relax, his body almost melting into the soft ground. The sky was high above him, cloudless, the deepest purple, almost black but not quite black, filled with millions and millions and millions of stars, and he wondered what it might be like to count them, those stars, and in his head he began to count them. *One . . . two . . . three . . .* And he found that if he picked any of the twinkling points of light and held that point fixed inside his mind, he could time the twinkling, and he could hear the music of the stars, music not unlike some of the songs he'd played before.

"Can you hear that?" he whispered.

And when she didn't answer, he rolled over on his side and

looked at her. She lay on her back, her hands behind her head, her body still and quiet save for the rise and fall of her chest as she breathed in and out. "Alexandria."

"She's sleeping," said a small voice. Oliver sat up. He saw no one.

"Right here," the voice said again. "Right here."

Oliver turned around, still sitting, pivoting easily on the slick wet grass. There was a child sitting on the grass next to him, and right away Oliver recognized him. "Thomas?"

The child nodded and shrugged at the same time.

"Are you real?" Oliver asked, reaching out a hand.

"No." Thomas said. "I died a long time ago, remember."

Oliver looked over at Alexandria, who still lay there peacefully. "Is *she* real?"

Thomas nodded. "Yes. She's real. But she's sleeping."

"How? She could never sleep before."

"She's always been sleeping, and now she's sleeping even more."

"I don't . . . Am I—"

"Crazy? Real?" Thomas smiled. "No. And in a manner of speaking."

"I don't understand."

"You're not meant to. We're never meant to understand."

A breeze blew across the hillside. It was a warm breeze. A cricket rubbed its legs together somewhere in the distance.

Oliver felt the stubble on his chin. "Okay," he said. He didn't know why he said it, but he did.

"You care about her," Thomas said.

Oliver nodded. "I do."

"She needs to go home."

"I know."

"You'll care about all of them, you know, if only briefly. And it's only meant to be brief—they're not meant to stay so long, not meant to go so deep, but sometimes it does happen."

"What do you mean?"

"I don't know. I'm not real. And even those that are can't stay forever, you see. All is ephemeral, Oliver, all of it. And it's your job now to make it last forever."

Oliver looked down. The pan flute was in his hand. He hadn't realized he'd brought it with him, but he was beginning to understand, even if he didn't really understand at all. "What do I do now?"

"Help her home."

"But where is that?"

Thomas didn't answer, but instead just turned and walked on down the hill. Weeks ago, Oliver might have called out or ran after him, or he might have dismissed the entire occurrence completely. But tonight he just stared as the young boy walked away and then, as if he'd never been there, altogether disappeared.

"What are you thinking?" Alexandria whispered.

Oliver was lying on his back, staring at the sky. He rolled over to find Alexandria on her side, looking at him. "Just about the stars," he said. "Can you hear it? The music?"

"Yeah," she said, "I think I can."

And it was as if neither heard the thunder or saw the flash of bluish-white ignite the sky. Clouds blew in above them, and they hardly noticed. And when those clouds opened up and the rain began to fall for the second time that night, soaking their clothes and their hair and their skin, they didn't say a word.

THE NEXT DAY SHOWED MANY signs of the previous night's violent storms. Shutters had been blown from windows, there were puddles here and puddles there, and in some places where the ground was unpaved, dirt had been transformed into a thick, gloppy mud. Shopfronts were missing signs, paint was beginning to peel off of doorposts and windowpanes, and a few crops had been killed by flooding.

Oliver played the morning song, another one he hadn't himself written, but that he had never played before in public. And after he played, the villagers set about to working, cleaning and building and repairing, and school was canceled so that every available person could lend a hand, but of course the children just played, splashing about in the puddles and tossing and kicking around mud, dirtying boots and galoshes and clothing much to the chagrin of their parents, who never seem to realize that children hardly know the meaning of the word chagrin and therefore are perfectly content to throw mud and make a mess for the sake of the jollification of even the worst situations. By midday, the cleanup was coming together nicely, and by the end of the afternoon, all the shop owners had begun to open their stores if only for the last remaining hours of the day—all shop owners, that is, save for the baker, who found himself frustrated and angry and suddenly enjoying some mysteriously delicious tartlets.

Oliver snatched an apple from a large bowl of fruit in the middle of the dining room table as he walked by. He exhaled deliberately onto the apple, polished its green skin on his shirt, bit into it. He'd forgotten to eat again today, caught up in his work just as the villagers were caught up in theirs, and it was only as he was walking briefly around the cottage to stretch his legs that he saw the bowl of fruit and realized he was hungry. He hadn't seen Alexandria since that morning—she was out in the village somewhere, he knew, doing what she could to help with the cleanup in her own invisible way.

Oliver had gone back to the music room, the apple between his teeth, and had picked up his pen when he heard a voice calling his name. He recognized two things: that the voice was his father's and that his father wasn't happy. His stomach turned a little and he pulled the apple out of his mouth.

"I'm right here, father," he called, walking back into the living room, still holding the pen and apple.

His father, instead of speaking, walked purposefully toward him, throwing a chair from the dining room table to the ground as he approached. His face was more than angry.

"Who is she?" his father said.

"Who?" Oliver was struck with mixed pangs of fear and hope. Had his father seen Alexandria? Did that mean he could help?

"I know what you're hiding." His father had stopped walking and stood less than a foot away. "A *girl*." He spat the words.

"I—"

"Don't lie to me, boy!" his father shouted. "You think I don't have people keeping an eye on you. Every single maid, cook and servant here reports back to *me*. I know your associating with a girl in this very house."

"What gives them that idea?"

"Eliza says she hears you talking at night, whispering in your room. And the kitchen staff says that food has gone missing nearly every single day for weeks."

So no one had actually seen her, then; Oliver was still the only one. And besides, the venom with which Oliver's father spat his words made it obvious that he would be anything but helpful. "So I talk to myself," he said. "It's how I think. It helps me write."

"I was here last night," his father said. "I was here to investigate these reports. And for a moment, I thought that perhaps they were wrong, because I couldn't hear you whispering. I didn't hear a sound. But then I opened your door . . . and do you know what I found?" He leaned in closer. "Nothing. The room was empty. You were gone."

"You were mistaken," Oliver said. "I was asleep—"

"You. Were. Not. There. Now tell me what you're up to." His father was growling.

"That's none of your business," Oliver said. He wanted to step back but held his ground.

"You have crossed the line this time. I humored you when you said you couldn't play. I coddled you when you were too weak to do what was required of you, but no more. From this day forward, you will have a servant by your side at all times, a servant that will report to me every day. I will not lose my place on the council because of your disobedience."

And then it all made sense to Oliver, and he realized that no matter what he wanted to do, only he had the power to do it, and he said, "You, father, are a selfish man. You can tell the council I quit. I don't need to play for them or anybody else."

"You can't—" his father said.

"I *can*," Oliver said, and the irony was that he *wanted* to play, but not like this. "And you can play your own damned flute."

The fist came at him fast and hard, and Oliver barely had time to register the pain on his cheek before he tasted warm metallic blood running deep inside his mouth. And yet he stood there, tall, and his feet barely moved at all when his father hit him a second time, and then a third. Instead, he dropped the pen. He brought the hand up firmly to his father's chest. He pushed. His other hand squeezed tight around the apple. Juice dripped around his fingers. "I want you out of my house," he said. "Now."

His father laughed. "You have no power—"

"It's my house. Get out."

Oliver pushed, not hard, and it wasn't without respect, but he pushed. His father stared at him, and Oliver stared back, and suddenly his father's self-assurance seemed to melt away. "We'll talk later," his father finally said. "We'll talk later." And then he left.

Oliver took a breath. He felt relieved, vindicated, scared. His hands trembled. His teeth chattered together. Sweat dripped down the base of his neck as he dropped to his knees. The nib had broken off the pen, and ink slowly poured from the opening, staining the wooden dining room floor. He still clenched the apple in his hand. It was more apple sauce than apple now.

He heard the door open again, and he looked up, certain that he couldn't hold his ground again. "I thought I told you—"

But it wasn't his father in the doorway.

"Alexandria."

She stumbled into the cottage, covered in mud and bruises, her skin pale, her hand against her stomach, gasping and retching desperately.

THE MOTHER JUMPS FROM HER chair, bumping her shoulder against the side of the father's head. The father starts to say something, but then he sees it too. The girl's eyelids blink open, and the eyes behind them are not lifeless, empty, but aware, confused, frightened. She turns her head about the room. The mother and the father speak to her, tell her they love her, and ask if she's alright. How does she feel? Does she remember what happened? And she wants to tell them that she does, sort of, and but it's all so ambiguous and what happened exactly, because she remembers part of it, but it's all so unclear, and what happened exactly? But she doesn't tell them. She can't speak. And she can't breathe at all. Her mouth moves, opens desperately. She gasps for air and makes these sort of low shallow shrieking sounds as she tries to suck air into her lungs. They hurt. It all hurts. She can't seem to make it work like she knows it should work.

The mother panics. What's happening, what's happening, she asks. The father runs to the doorway, into the corridor, calling for help. Someone help. She's awake, but she can't breathe.

The old German doctor is nearby, and he and a nurse hurry into the room. He says to get them out of there, the parents, and to bring him some tools. He says something about a trachea or a collapsed lung, something about oxygen and the brain. Get them out of here, dammit, I said get them out of here.

The mother screams and cries. The father asks panicked questions. The nurse pulls them both toward the door. They can't be in here right now, not while the doctor is trying to work.

Another nurse pushes a cart into the room beside the bed, and on the cart are a variety of tubes and cutting instruments. The doctor wants to ask if they're sterile, but he knows they're probably not— there's no time to sterilize anything here anymore, and infection is the least of their worries now anyway. He looks for a scalpel but can't seem to find it. Where's the scalpel? They give him a razor blade. It's all they have right now. It doesn't matter, the razor will have to do.

An hour passes. The nurse asks the parents to come back into the room. Their daughter is lying on the table, a plastic tube sticking out of her throat, attached to nothing. She's breathing now, but it's short and shallow and loud, and the sound is coming from the tube. Her airway is beginning to inflame, he tells them, and there's only so much he can do. And also a vessel near her spleen has ruptured, and he's fixed it, but it will probably happen again and again, and she may bleed out any time now. Or she may not. He just doesn't know. She's back in the coma, though, he tells them, which is a good thing because she'll need less oxygen this way. And get that damned IV out of her arm, he tells a nurse, we ran out of fluids hours ago.

FOR THE MOMENT, ALEXANDRIA SEEMED to be okay. The pain in her stomach had subsided, and she was breathing easily again. She sat in a chair in the dining room, and Oliver handed her a glass of water.

Alexandria began to gulp the water, but Oliver put a hand on her shoulder. "Slowly."

She ignored him, downing the glass in seconds. "Your face," she said, looking up at him. "You're hurt."

Oliver raised a hand to his mouth. The blood was still a little wet. He had forgotten the encounter with his father when he saw Alexandria, but now his lip and cheek began to sting, and he was once again aware of the metallic taste of blood in his mouth. "It's nothing," he said, reaching for a napkin on the table and holding it to his mouth. "What about you? What happened?"

She was quiet, her eyes searching for something far away. She held out the empty glass, still thirsty. "I don't know, exactly. I was out exploring. I went into the forest, because I realized I hadn't been there since, well you know, since I got here. So I went in—not very far in or anything, not very deep, just past the edge—and for a minute, I was home again."

Oliver took the empty glass, meaning to fill it. "Home?"

"Sort of. I was in a room. And there were people there. And . . . and at first I didn't know who they were, but they seemed so happy to see me, and I realized, they're my parents. They're waiting for me, Oliver."

Oliver sat there, holding the empty glass.

"And I wanted to speak to them, to tell them I love them, and that I'm okay, that I'm right here, but I couldn't speak. It was like, like, like my body was there with them, in the room, and I think it was a hospital room, like I'm sick, and but . . . and but my mind wasn't there, because I couldn't speak, couldn't talk, couldn't tell them that I remembered them. And then I couldn't remember where I'd been, like I forgot about here and you in the same way that I've forgotten them, and I felt like I was in so many places, but I didn't actually know where any of those places were. And I couldn't . . . I couldn't think. I couldn't inhale. And my chest hurt, and my stomach. And then my parents were gone, and I wasn't even sure if they were my parents anymore—but they were—and there was this old man, a doctor, and I know he's a doctor because I've seen him before around the city. And then—"

She was talking so fast, exhausting herself, and Oliver realized he was still holding the empty glass. He rose and walked into the kitchen, refilling the glass with water. He handed it to her. "And then?"

"And then I was back here, at your door." She took the glass, sipping this time. "But they're out there, Oliver, and so am I. Part of me is with them, and I think, if I don't get back there, back to my world, I'm going to die."

You care about her.

I do.

You'll care about all about all of them, you know?

. . .

Help her home.

. . .

Help her home, Oliver.

They sat alone in the house for many hours, talking about what to do and what they were meant to do. Oliver knew she was right—she had to return to her own world. He had known it since he first found her in the woods that night, trapped in the fire, calling for help. But only now did he understand that she was still trapped. She was trapped here with him. He hadn't saved her yet.

THE FOREST HAD NOT BEEN nearly so dark the last time Oliver had ventured into it, he mused. Then again, maybe it had. It had been so long ago, or at least so it seemed, when he had run from his bed and into the woods, barefoot and half-naked, to find the source of the desperate cries for help. If he were to say that he weren't scared, then or now, he'd be lying.

"What are you thinking about?"

"Nothing." And so he lied, both to himself and to Alexandria. He lied, but he fooled no one, and everyone has a right to try to fool themselves sometimes.

The forest didn't have a name. It was just The Forest as far as anybody was concerned. Few ever entered it, fewer still had ever been as far as Oliver had, and certainly nobody ever had passed beyond it. It was not particularly large—just a collection of trees and brush surrounding the village and the fields—and one could even see the sea beyond it from the top of the highest hill. And notes when viewed on paper don't seem so very large, either, but when we let ourselves inside the music, it's easy to get lost in them.

Oliver wasn't sure how long they'd been walking, or even

where they were going, but he knew that if Alexandria were going to find a way home, it would happen here. This is where she'd entered the world, and these woods were where she'd been when she'd almost left earlier that day.

They'd left the village in the late evening, just as the sun was hiding behind the tall side of the mountains, casting the village in the breathtaking sanguine glow of diffused light reflecting off the distant snow. The evening was always most beautiful the day after a violent storm.

As they walked, silent save for their footsteps crunching leaves and snapping twigs on the soft ground, Oliver fingered the pan flute in his pocket. He'd finished his first original song today, just before he'd gotten up to stretch his legs and get that apple, but he hadn't played it for the villagers that evening—no one had come to take him to the square.

"I've been wondering something," Alexandria said, breaking his rumination.

A bird or something chortled in the distance. "What have you been wondering?"

They didn't stop walking, and she didn't look at him, but rather at the sky, which was only partially visible beyond the leafy canopy. "If the sun circles around the mountains, then what about the moon?"

Oliver looked at the sky, too. They kept walking to an unknown destination. "What about it?"

"It doesn't circle. It's just there."

"Yeah. It's just there."

The moon was large and full. It was always large and full and bright, just there in the sky, shining down above them, upon them, through the sky and the trees, surrounded by stars.

Alexandria nodded. It was just there.

And then the sky erupted. A giant creature swept in as if out of nowhere. It rushed by with a whoosh and the air grew hot around them. Oliver recognized the beast immediately. It was long, the size from its head to the tip of its tail at least as long as the village square. On its back were massive wings, like ten of Oliver's bed sheets stitched together, except that these were much thicker than bed sheets, like leather and canvas, and between the wings, spikes, white, like ivory breaking through the scaly skin. And the beast's breath was fire, scorching the air and the trees as the creature loosed a deafening roar. It never stopped moving, just swooped past out of nowhere, grasping Alexandria in one of its massive claws—claws like talons a thousand times too large—and disappeared into the forest, beyond the blazing trees.

Oliver spun in circles. "Alexandria." His throat was dry and his voice was hoarse. Smoke filled the wood around him. He choked on the thick, burning air, doubled over, fighting for breath. His hands on his knees, he raised his head, scanning the woods around him searching desperately for he didn't know what. A weapon. A person. Something.

Oliver ran as fast as he could, as hard as he could, and with as much will as he had ever done anything in his life. Nothing made sense to him. The person he cared about more than anyone in his entire life had been spirited away by a creature that couldn't exist. And it didn't matter how much he ran after them, they were gone. All was darkness—even the trees seemed to have disappeared, the forest itself ceasing to exist around him. Could it be that she had gone for good? Was this the manner in which she would exit this world, in the claws of some impossible beast?

"She's not gone," said a voice from behind him. A deep, masculine, kindly voice.

Oliver turned. "What?"

"I said that your lady is not gone," said the man. It was the same man who Oliver had seen in these same woods before, the man who had announced that he would save the village from the dragon, the same dragon that had disappeared then and reappeared now. And Oliver still didn't know what a dragon was, except that it was mammoth and breathed fire and stole innocent young women into the night. And here now was a man who fought dragons, dressed in the same suit of gleaming armor he had been wearing then, a sword drawn at his side. "We can save her."

"How?"

"We can defeat the dragon. You and I, but not alone. Never alone, you see. No, no, we'll need more men to help us."

"More men? Who? How many?" And there wasn't *time* to find more men. They needed to save her now.

"I do not know. One more. Ten. A legion. It's never the same, you see."

"Never the same. But what does that mean?"

The man sheathed his sword, hung his helmeted head low. "Nay," the man said, and Oliver didn't know what that meant, "but I lie. It's always the same. Every night, and for all eternity, I fight this odious beast. I hunt it, and sometimes it hunts me, and I stab my sword into its sordid heart and it falls, it always falls, you see, and sometimes I've time to cut its head off to prove to myself it's dead, and then I awake, and the bastard returns the next night. And the next. And the next."

Oliver leaned forward, lowered his brow. "Awake. You said you wake up. What did you mean by that?"

"It doesn't matter," the man said. "It doesn't matter."

"It *does*, though," Oliver said. "To me. And to the girl the dragon took away."

"It doesn't matter," the man said again. "I cannot stop it."

"Then give me your sword."

"Pardon?"

"Give me your sword. I've got to get her back. *I'll* kill the dragon."

The man's hand went to his weapon. "You?"

"Yes. I have to."

The man chuckled, and given the circumstances, it was both, Oliver thought, a bizarre thing to do and at the same time unsurprising. "Well," said the man, "this is indeed new. What is your name, young squire."

Oliver didn't know what squire meant, but he said, "Oliver."

"Well, then," the man said, and he brought his hands to his helmet and took it off, and he was younger than Oliver would have expected, only about Oliver's age, in fact, and his eyes were wide and his smile lopsided, and the man held the helmet under one arm and drew his sword with the other and brought it down toward Oliver, and Oliver flinched, but the man only tapped him lightly on the shoulder. "I anoint thee, Sir Oliver."

Oliver didn't know what any of that meant. The air was still. And the trees were still on fire, Oliver's throat still dry. He blinked tears out of red eyes. He coughed. Nothing happened. "Now what?" he said.

"Now," the man said, but he let the word hang. He cocked his head to the side, seemed to chew on his lower lip like he was listening for something. And then he grinned. "Now, I say good luck."

Oliver stared at the young man. "I don't—" And then there was a roar, almost like a shriek, and Oliver was in the air, trapped in the talons of the fire-breathing beast. And Oliver could still hear the young man on the ground, chuckling and chuckling and chuckling, and the laughter faded in the distance.

The creature ascended, turning toward the great ocean. "Oh dear," someone said.

Oliver twisted in the creature's grasp. In the other claw was the other man whom Oliver had seen that first time in the woods. The fat man. And he was again naked, except that this time, instead of a flower pinned to his chest, he wore a pleated red cummerbund. "Oh dear," he said again. "This always seems to happen."

"Who are you?" Oliver said, not exactly surprised. "What are you doing here?"

The fat man looked at him. He twisted, pulling an arm free from the beast's claw so that he could wipe a bead of sweat off his forehead. "Oh, you know," the man said, "just sitting here, naked and all."

And then the man was gone, just like last time.

The dragon opened his massive claw, and Oliver fell into the ocean.

"Oliver."

He sank into the abyss, the water engulfing him. He couldn't swim, couldn't see, couldn't move. The world was black and direction was meaningless. It was cold, dark, quiet. Oliver was alone and lost.

"Oliver."

"Thomas? Where are you?"

"It doesn't matter. I'm still not real."

"Thomas, I shouldn't have let you die."

"There was nothing you could have done for me, Oliver. Nothing lasts forever. Nothing."

"Who are these people? What are these things?"

"I suppose," said Thomas, and Oliver felt himself sinking deeper into the darkness, "that I should put it like this. There are people, not so far away, and they live in a whole different world. And sometimes, when they sleep, they dream."

"Dream?"

"You won't understand, not exactly, but you're not meant to understand. And anyway."

"What else? Are they real?"

"The people are real," Thomas said, and Oliver still couldn't see him. "In a manner of speaking. They come here sometimes, and you are very special, because you get to see them and talk to them and play with them. But they're not meant to stay forever, you see. Sometimes, they might become tethered to this world, like the girl, but that isn't supposed to happen."

"You mean Alexandria."

"Yes, her. But they can't last forever, Oliver. Not really. They have their own lives, and they must always return to them. But you can still immortalize them."

Oliver was floating, neither sinking nor rising, neither breathing nor drowning, neither living nor dying. He reached into his pocket. He understood. "And what about the other things? The dragon or the vehicle from before? Are they real?"

"Not like the people."

"And this other world—where is it?"

"Not far."

And Oliver was standing just at the edge of the ocean now, right where the forest meets the shore. The sky was full of stars, and the stars reflected on the water like millions of tiny memories, distorted by the ripples and the waves. Thomas stood in front of him. "Just over there," Thomas said, whispering, and nodded off into the distance, toward the mountains. And then he dove into the water, the stars parting to let him through, and then they closed again behind him.

"Well," the voice was deep, "I am impressed."

Oliver turned around. He'd lost his shoes somehow. He could feel the cool sand beneath his toes. There was the man in the silver armor, his helmet back on his head. And just beyond him on the beach was the dragon, just standing there, massive and unmoving. "What's going on?" Oliver said.

"Your lady has tamed the dragon," the man said, gesturing at the beast behind him.

And there she was, Alexandria, sitting on the creature's scale-covered back, which rose and fell as it breathed.

"Alexandria! How did you—"

She shrugged. "Don't ask me."

The young man in the armor laughed again. "Impressed, indeed," he said.

Oliver walked up to the gigantic creature. It roared quietly, but not violently, as he grabbed scales, climbing up its hide. When he reached its back, he crawled over to Alexandria. "You need to go home now," he said.

She nodded. "What about you?"

Oliver smiled. "I'm going to play the music," he said. "Every morning and every evening. And during the day, I'll write it. And at night I'll come back here."

She nodded again. "Will I see you again?"

"I think so," he said. "I think you can return for a little while, now and then, if you'd like."

"I would like that."

"Goodbye, then, for now." He kissed her forehead, and then he turned and climbed down.

"Wait. How am I going to get home?"

Oliver turned back toward her. He smiled. And then he walked over to the front of the dragon, and it lowered its head onto the sand. Oliver whispered into its ear and it snorted, smoke rising from its nostrils. Oliver looked at Alexandria. "Hold on," he said.

He stepped back, joining the man in the silver armor, and the beast stood up on its legs, shook its shoulders, snorted again, and took off into the sky. Oliver and the man watched as it flew off into the distance, Alexandria on its back, and disappeared behind the mountains.

"Very impressed, indeed."

Oliver turned, just in time to see the man fade away.

As Oliver made his way back through the woods to the village, alone, but not lonely, and certainly not lost, the naked man appeared again in front of him.

"Excuse me," Oliver said, "but you always seem to be quite naked."

The man looked down. He was wearing the cummerbund *and* the flower this time, and he was holding a leather briefcase. "Oh my."

An hour later, Oliver could see the village as he made his way over the hill. The sun was just beginning to come out from behind the mountains, and there were people gathering in the square. Oliver reached into his pocket, feeling for the pan flute. It was still there, smooth and real and reassuring, and Oliver had a new song that he thought just might last forever.

THE DOCTOR CAN'T BELIEVE IT, but the girl seems just fine. He's removed the tube from her neck and stitched the tissue, and she's talking and laughing, and he doesn't think there's any internal bleeding. She's been awake for hours now, and he doesn't know how to explain it, but it doesn't matter. He doesn't want to. He pats the girl on the shoulder and shakes the father's hand and says he'll be around if they need him, and he wanders out of the room and into the corridor with a headache, desperate for a cigarette or something.

The father tells a joke, something ridiculous and not entirely unfunny, and the mother hugs her daughter again, and she must have hugged her at least twenty times by now, but it doesn't get old, the hugging, does it?

And the girl doesn't exactly remember everything, but she's awake and happy. And she knows her parents and she knows her city, and she loves everything so very much. She's hungry and is there food, she asks.

And the mother hugs the father, and he looks down at her, his beautiful wife, and grins, his bearded cheeks stretching from ear to ear, and kisses her and pulls her in close with one arm. He pulls his daughter in with the other, and they look at each other, the three of them, and laugh, and the father says that there must be something to eat somewhere, some bread and some cheese or something, and he'll check with one of the nurses. Right now, he's happy she, his daughter, is with them.

And but all is ephemeral, and sometimes there can be no resolution. And so outside the hospital room, outside the window and above the city, large metal beasts, not unlike hellish man-made dragons, fly by on ferrous wings. And their bellies open up, and they drop fire from their mouths. And the ground explodes in a thousand different places. The world erupts. The buildings that still stand won't stand much longer. And the bombs take the city a second time. And the rubble takes the people.

And somewhere not so very far away, Oliver thinks he sees Alexandria, but it's only for a moment. He raises the instrument to his lips.

ABOUT THE AUTHOR

Shawn was born in San Diego, California, in 1990, where he lived until he was seven.

In high school, he won several awards both as a writer for and editor-in-chief of his student newspaper, prompting him to study journalism before deciding that his passion for writing was better directed at fiction.

Shawn currently lives in Helena, MT, with his fiancé.

OTHER WORKS BY SHAWN MIHALIK

The Flute Player

Brand-Changing Day: A Novel

Particles: A Novel